THE BEAR WENT OVER THE MOUNTAIN

By STEVEN ANDERSON

Illustrated by TIM PALIN

CANTATA
LEARNING

MANKATO, MINNESOTA

WWW.CANTATALEARNING.COM

CANTATA LEARNING

MANKATO, MINNESOTA

Published by Cantata Learning
1710 Roe Crest Drive
North Mankato, MN 56003
www.cantatalearning.com

Library of Congress Control Number: 2014957031
978-1-63290-276-4 (hardcover/CD)
978-1-63290-428-7 (paperback/CD)
978-1-63290-470-6 (paperback)

The Bear Went over the Mountain by Steven Anderson
Illustrated by Tim Palin

Book design, Tim Palin Creative
Editorial direction, Flat Sole Studio
Executive musical production and direction, Elizabeth Draper
Music arranged and produced by Steven C Music

Printed in the United States of America.

VISIT

WWW.CANTATALEARNING.COM/ACCESS-OUR-MUSIC

TO SING ALONG TO THE SONG

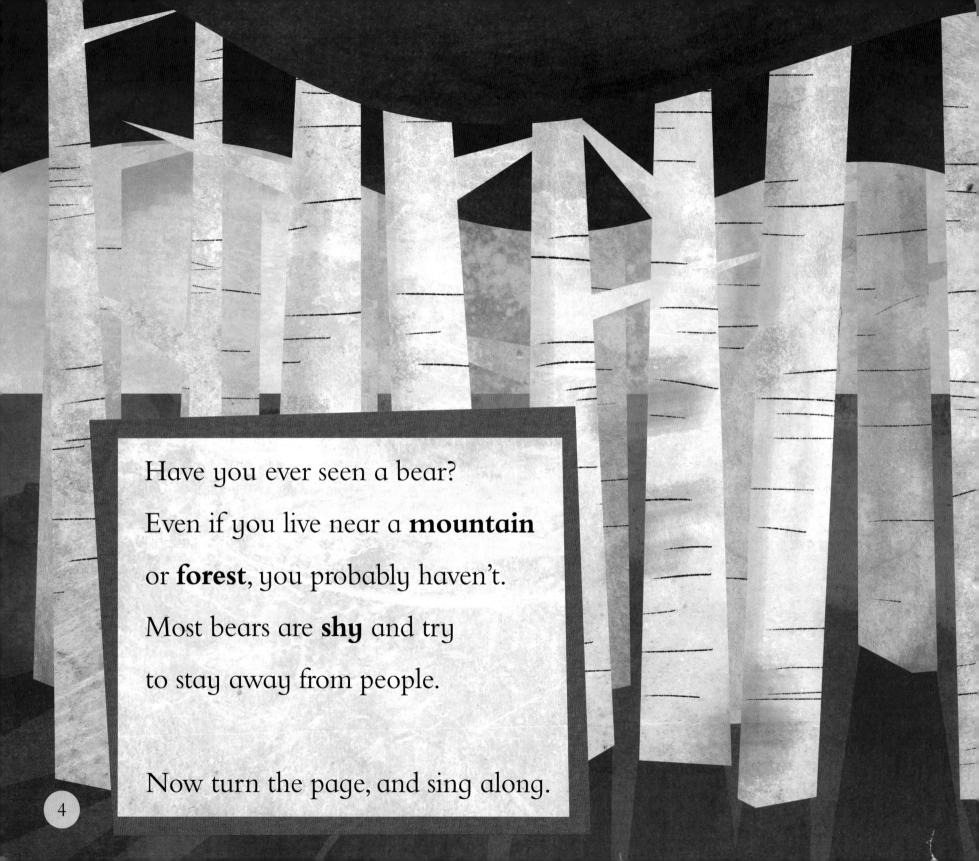

Have you ever seen a bear?

Even if you live near a **mountain**

or **forest**, you probably haven't.

Most bears are **shy** and try

to stay away from people.

Now turn the page, and sing along.

The bear went over the mountain.

The bear went over the mountain.

The bear went over the mountain

To see what he could see.

To see what he could see.

To see what he could see.

The other side of the mountain.

The other side of the mountain.

The other side of the mountain
Was all that he could see.

10

He found another bear there.
He found another bear there.

He found another bear there
Who could have been his **twin**.

13

Who could have
been his twin.

Who could have
been his twin.

He found another bear there.
He found another bear there.

He found another bear there
And off they went to play.

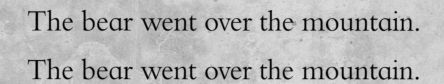

The bear went over the mountain.

The bear went over the mountain.

The bear went over the mountain

To see what he could see.

The other side of the mountain.

The other side of the mountain.

The other side of the mountain

Was all that he could see.

SONG LYRICS
The Bear Went over the Mountain

The bear went over the mountain.
The bear went over the mountain.

The bear went over the mountain
To see what he could see.

To see what he could see.
To see what he could see.

The other side of the mountain.
The other side of the mountain.

The other side of the mountain
Was all that he could see.

He found another bear there.
He found another bear there.

He found another bear there
Who could have been his twin.

Who could have
been his twin.

Who could have
been his twin.

He found another bear there.
He found another bear there.

He found another bear there
And off they went to play.

The bear went over the mountain.
The bear went over the mountain.

The bear went over the mountain
To see what he could see.

The other side of the mountain.
The other side of the mountain.

The other side of the mountain
Was all that he could see.

The Bear Went over the Mountain

Americana
Steven C Music

Verse 1 (ABA)

1. The bear went o-ver the moun-tain. The bear went o-ver the moun-tain. The
The oth-er side of the moun-tain. The oth-er side of the moun-tain. The

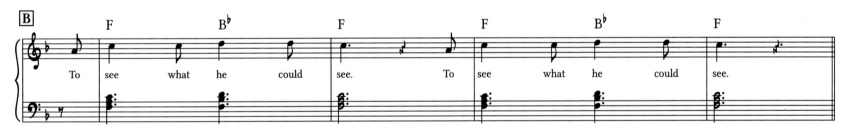

bear went o-ver the moun-tain To see what he could see.
oth-er side of the moun-tain Was all what that he could see.

To see what he could see. To see what he could see.

Verse 2 (ABA)

A. He found another bear there.
He found another bear there.
He found another bear there
Who could have been his twin.

B. Who could have been his twin.
Who could have been his twin.

A. He found another bear there.
He found another bear there.
He found another bear there
And off they went to play.

Verse 3 (AA)

A. The bear went over the mountain.
The bear went over the mountain.
The bear went over the mountain
To see what he could see.

A. The other side of the mountain.
The other side of the mountain.
The other side of the mountain
Was all that he could see.

GLOSSARY

forest—a large area thickly covered with trees and plants; forests are also called woodlands.

mountain—a very tall hill

shy—easily frightened or startled

twins—two children born at the same time and to the same parents; some twins look the same and some twins look different.

GUIDED READING ACTIVITIES

1. Why do you think the bear wanted to go over the mountain? What did the bear see?

2. Come up with 3 other things the bear might see over the mountain.

3. Pretend you are the bear. Instead of going over the mountain go inside of a cave. What would you see?

TO LEARN MORE

Aboff, Marcie. *Do You Really Want to Meet a Polar Bear?* Mankato, MN: Amicus Illustrated, 2015.

Guillain, Charlotte. *Goldiclucks and the Three Bears*. Chicago: Capstone Raintree, 2013.

Kolpin, Molly. *Grizzly Bears*. North Mankato, MN: Capstone Press, 2013.

Kukowski, Alex. *Bears*. Minneapolis: ABDO Publishing Company, 2015.